I0726958

STORIES

OF
THE VEIL

LUNA

LUNA

THE VEILED

PEPPER MCGRAW

PMG Publishing

Cover Art:
Design by Definition

Inside Images:
Freeskyblue | Dreamstime

ISBN 978-1-951247-19-5

Edited by J.L. Troughton
PMG Publishing

CONTENTS

Chapter 1   1
Chapter 2   19
Chapter 3   39
Chapter 4   61
Chapter 5   79
Chapter 6   95
Excerpt   113

Thank you for reading   117
Other Books by Pepper   119
Anthologies & Collections   121
About the Author   123

CHAPTER 1

LUNA VERUSHI GLARED at the arrogant Fae who seemed to think he could boss her around just because he was having a crisis over the fact they were mates.

Not that he'd acknowledged their bond or anything.

Oh, no, he'd been too busy lecturing her to bother with something as important as a mating.

Which was absolutely fine with her.

She didn't need a mate and certainly not one who thought he knew what was best for her.

"You're not going," he growled for what had to be the seventh time since he'd knocked on her lodging's door that morning.

She didn't even know his name because he hadn't bothered to introduce himself.

Instead, he'd taken one look at her and started ranting about staying behind and letting him handle the situation.

As if he even knew what the situation was.

Beyond what everyone in Faerie already knew, of course—that the Veils had fallen, then reformed as solid barriers, no longer open for travel between the realms. In the process, thousands of Fae had been trapped on the mortal side of the Veils, cut off entirely from Faerie.

Beyond that, he shouldn't even know that she had a plan—no matter that it was a rather risky one—let alone the specifics of it. Even more perplexing was how he'd managed to find her in the first place.

There was only one other person who knew what Luna had discovered and surely she wouldn't—

Luna whirled and glared at the interfering Fae. "Did Zara send you?"

He stopped ranting and faced her, eyebrow raised. "Do you honestly believe she should have just let you carry on with your reckless plan on your own, with no backup? Is that what you think?"

Luna rolled her eyes. "It isn't reckless. I've done all the calculations and I have the entire natural world to back me up."

"Look, I'm sure you're quite talented, but in the mortal world, you cannot possibly expect to retain full access to whatever tiny bits of earth magic you happen to have here in Faerie."

Luna gasped. "Tiny bits of earth magic? Why you—" She barely caught the reins of her magic as it surged in reaction to her fury.

No.

He wasn't worth expelling the energy to teach him a lesson, no matter how tempting it was.

She whirled around, grabbed the last of her things, shoved them into her satchel and closed it tight.

Swinging it over her shoulder, she headed for the door.

"And just where do you think you're going?" He followed her out of her room and down the stairs into the main room of the inn where she'd been staying.

She ignored him because honestly, she did not need this additional stress on the morning of her grand adventure.

She already had no idea how this trip would go— whether she would make it to her intended destination and even if she did, whether she would ever be able to return.

Perhaps she'd be trapped just like the many other missing Fae.

Worst case scenario, she'd be trapped somewhere far from her brother.

Best case, she'd find him quickly and at least be with part of her family while cut off from Faerie.

Because of its unpredictability and inherent risks, this entire adventure had her anxiety soaring, especially since Zara had been called away at the last minute to assist in a royal healing, leaving Luna to make this trip on her own.

She would have waited for Zara, but Luna had been tracking this roaming Veil all over Faerie for an entire year, and somehow she always managed to just barely miss it.

She couldn't afford to skip this opportunity, even knowing she'd probably fail again, because there was always the possibility that her calculations were actually correct this time and she would arrive at the perfect moment.

It was actually a bit of a terrifying thought—that she might, by the vagaries of fate, catch the Veil the one time Zara wasn't with her, and would have no choice but to take the risk and travel through it alone.

Zara had to know that Luna wouldn't wait and risk missing the Veil again, which was probably why she'd sent to Luna this infuriating, overbearing, condescending Fae, who was full of arrogant assumptions and a ridiculous belief that he could dictate her actions.

Worse yet was the fact that he turned out to be her mate.

Fate could be such a vindictive, hateful creature sometimes.

"Are you even listening to me?"

Luna didn't answer. It wasn't worth attempting to reason with him as he obviously lacked the logic gene.

She stormed out of the inn and set off down the path toward the woods where her window of opportunity was winding down.

"You need to stop and think, Luna," the Fae insisted as he followed her. "This isn't safe. If you wish for someone to test your theory, I will happily do so. It would be an honor, but you cannot do this yourself. You are of Faerie and you need to remain here. We cannot risk the loss of yet another—"

"Another what? Female?" She continued down the path, refusing to pause for even a moment to address his outrageous claims. "There are plenty of females trapped on the wrong side of the Veils and I'm going to find them and help them come home if they wish."

"It isn't your job, Luna —"

"Stop saying my name as if you know who I am."

"I know exactly who you are. You are Zara's little sister and the youngest sister of Mitaru, a Guardian trapped in the mortal realm when the Veils fell."

"Congratulations. That tells you exactly nothing." She brushed some branches aside as she entered the woods and began to run, a feeling of urgency creeping upon her, as if the window was closing faster than she'd expected.

"I can assure you, Mitaru would not thank me for allowing his baby sister to take such risks."

"Mitaru would support me as he always did and he would trust me. Do not speak as if you know anything of our relationship." She practically flew down the path, furious that he continued to follow her, arguing the entire way.

"Very well then. I'll speak of what I know of our relationship instead. You are my mate, Luna." The Fae kept pace with her as he spoke emphatically of a mating she now wanted no part of.

"Good luck with that one." She raced faster and faster, leaping over obstacles, the beacon calling her ramping up in power.

"Luna, please, listen to me."

They burst into a clearing and Luna stumbled to a halt.

There it was.

The roaming Veil that she'd been tracking for a year.

Her last hope.

"Finally," she whispered.

"It's even smaller than I expected," the Fae murmured at her side.

She'd almost forgotten he was there.

"How in the name of Faerie are you planning to breach it?"

She shrugged. "The Sorenalaya never seem to have any trouble."

"Because they're insubstantial. They can squeeze through the tiniest pinprick. We, however, are made of flesh and bone and could never fit through that minuscule portion of the Veil."

"Not we. Me."

"Absolutely not. If you think I'm going to allow—"

"Excuse me? You're insane if you think you can dictate anything to me." She pushed her other arm through the second strap of her satchel, settling it more firmly on her back, and focused on the spaces to either side of the Veil. "I suggest you stand back."

Whatever he was going to say was lost in the rumble that began beneath their feet, the land lifting and subsiding in a great wave that split into two directions and ended about three feet to the left and right of the minuscule, roaming Veil.

Everything fell to stillness, then in the quiet, two bushes sprang to life on either side of the Veil.

Rising from the ground, they went from brown to green to fully abloom in purple and white flowers in a fraction of an instant.

The tiny pocket of space that had broken free from the Veils countless years before, that had not been impacted by their fall or their reformation as closed gateways, reacted immediately.

It began to turn and twist until it faced both bushes at the same time, then reached toward them, a tiny pocket in space stretching and growing until it became a narrow window through which Luna planned to travel.

The Fae's jaw dropped. "How did you do that?"

"I left instructions for my sister on the table in my house in case I do not return. See that she gets them, would you?" With that, Luna took a running leap and dove headfirst through the roaming Veil.

At the very last second, something caught her ankle on the Faerie side, but her momentum was so great it simply pulled whatever had hold of her through the Veil with her.

Luna landed in a heap on the mortal side, stunned to find herself lying on her back when logic dictated she should have landed on her stomach.

Twisty, tricky roaming Veil to somehow turn her entire body—or perhaps it turned the world—and leave her blinking at the stars in the sky above, pinned under the weight of an obnoxious, overbearing Fae who had somehow latched on and traveled with her.

Shoving him off her, she scrambled up and was gratified to realize, after a quick glance around in the darkness lit only by the light of the stars and moon, that there were no mortals in their vicinity. "I cannot believe you! The least you can do is give me your name before deciding to stalk me through the Veil."

The Fae lunged to his feet and sketched a sweeping bow in her direction. "Tarek Evaria, at your service." He held the position for a long moment, making Luna's breath catch in her throat as his dark eyes remained on hers.

Dragging in a deep breath, she took another giant step backward while attempting to shake off the effects of his compelling gaze. "Look, Tarek, I did not ask for you to be at my service so don't—"

"Luna," Tarek said, straightening quickly, eyes wide. "Stop moving."

"For Fae's sake! Is every word out of your mouth a command? Have you never heard the word please? Or perhaps a 'Would you consider?' That would be a nice change—to be asked instead of commanded."

"Seriously, just step toward me." He reached out an arm and beckoned her closer.

Luna threw her hands in the air. "It's like I'm talking to air." She moved to step back again and Tarek lunged forward, catching her with a pop of air magic that flung her into his arms with such force, they both ended up on the ground again.

This time, she was on top. "Are you insane?"

"What kind of idiotic Fae lands in another world

and doesn't even bother to take in her surroundings?" Tarek lunged to his feet, hauling her up with him in a massive display of strength that made her heart hammer in her chest.

"Well, excuse me. It happens to be a little dark out here!" She must have miscalculated the timing as she'd expected to arrive mid-morning. Instead, the sun had not yet risen. Either that or it was the roaming Veil again, not just twisting the world when they traveled through it, but twisting time too.

Tarek moved away from where she'd been standing, then set her on her feet and whirled her around so she stood with her back to his chest. "That should have just made you take more care, especially when you knew we'd be landing here!" He swept an arm out to encompass the view in front of them.

Luna's breath caught in her throat. "The canyon of the tribes," she whispered and wondered if the Havasupai and others still made their homes there.

A glance around showed her they'd landed on a ledge, the majestic wall of the canyon rising at their back, a path on their left leading up while another to their right headed down, and directly across, mere steps from where they'd originally landed, the cavernous canyon of the tribes stretched before them.

Tarek was right.

It might be dark out, but it certainly wasn't pitch

black. The sky had enough light that dawn couldn't be far off, meaning she should never have missed the canyon she'd almost backed into, not that she would ever admit that to Tarek.

Besides, if he hadn't insisted on joining her, she'd never have been distracted or trying to back away from him in the first place.

In other words, this was definitely his fault.

"You see?" he demanded.

Luna rolled her eyes at the superior tone in his voice. Then, just to aggravate him, she gave a quick hop of excitement and squealed, "I do see! Can you believe it? I've only ever been here once before—and that was hundreds of years ago—but it was so majestic, I've always wanted to come back. I cannot believe the roaming Veil brought us here."

"Hold on a minute. Are you saying you didn't even know where we'd end up when you went through the Veil?" Tarek demanded incredulously.

"Of course, I didn't know. No one knows where a Veil like that will lead. They're completely unpredictable, hopping around, visiting different places. That's why they're called roaming Veils." She'd never have thought she'd be grateful for their unpredictability, yet here she was, profoundly grateful to be at this site once more.

"What kind of idiot dives through a tiny pocket in

space without knowing where they'll land?" Tarek exploded behind her. "Are you insane? We could have both ended up falling to our deaths!"

Luna whirled to face him, hands on her hips. "Well, no one invited you, you pompous hitchhiker!"

"Excuse me? What in the world is a hitchhiker?"

Luna threw her arms up and stomped past him, intending to leave him behind, but his accusations rang in her head, goading her past endurance. "And another thing!" She whirled to face him again. "What kind of idiot comes into the mortal world dressed like that?" She waved an arm at his ridiculous garb.

"What are you talking about?"

"You look Fae!"

"I am Fae."

"Yes, and now you're obviously Fae in the mortal realm!"

"What's your point?"

"My point is you need to look mortal."

"Why in the name of Faerie would I want that?"

She just stared at him.

"We are the immortal Fae! Do you honestly believe the mortals are a threat? To us? Besides, we can just use our glamour."

"First of all, even mortals can be a threat in significant enough numbers, Tarek. Secondly, the mortal world has changed in ways we cannot even imagine.

Thousands of Fae crossed over in a moment. It's completely illogical to assume the mortals witnessed none of the crossings and that our glamour will still work on those witnesses. Witnesses who have now seen the truth."

Tarek let out a huff of exasperation. "You know as well as I do, Luna, that the mortals excel at burying their heads in the sand. I'm sure within moments, they had a logical explanation for the crossing and it's doubtful that explanation had anything to do with the Fae."

"That's a really big leap in logic. Besides, it bears repeating—in significant enough numbers, anything can become a threat. And in this case, those numbers, at least to the mortals, were the Fae appearing out of nowhere. So, assuming you want to survive this trip, we need to be traveling incognito—thank goodness no one was around to see our arrival—which means you're just going to have to look the part, like I do. Time to Veil your Fae–ness." With that, she waved a hand and the threads holding together Tarek's very traditional, Fae clothing unraveled.

*T*arek let out a choked sound of horror and tried to catch his tunic and trousers as they disintegrated from his form, but there was no stopping the process once begun.

The threads completely unraveled, then came back together again, weaving into a new pattern on his body, somehow thicker on his bottom half and lighter on the top while tighter pretty much everywhere.

It all happened so quickly he went from clothed to naked to clothed again in an instant.

He was almost afraid to look, then wished he hadn't. "What are these?" He tugged at the blue material encasing his legs.

"They're called jeans."

"They're horribly constricting." He desperately wanted to readjust himself, but resisted the urge.

Luna grinned. "They're very popular here. You'll fit right in."

"What about this?" He fingered the extremely light-weight, black tunic he was now wearing.

"It's a t-shirt. Oh, wait. Hats!" She pulled her satchel from her back and reached inside, dragging out two fuzzy, long things that in no way resembled hats.

She tossed one to Tarek and pulled the other over her head, taking care to hide her ears.

"You're joking, right?" Tarek stared down at the

black, fuzzy thing he now held and vowed there was no power in any of the realms that would make him wear it.

"What? It's adorable." Luna snatched it from his hands and went to shove it on his head, but he darted away.

"Absolutely not." He whirled to face her, marveling that she didn't feel completely ridiculous wearing her own version of what she'd given him. Then again, on her, he had to admit it was downright adorable.

Her reddish-brown hair was completely hidden beneath a white and fluffy head. There really was no other way to describe it.

It had eyes and a pink nose and ears, plus two long flaps that covered her exquisite, Fae ears and dangled past her shoulders. A closer look revealed those flaps ended in what appeared to be actual paws.

She was wearing an animal's head on top of her own and she had animal paws resting on her bosom.

And she thought this was going to help them blend in.

Tarek shook his head, worried that perhaps his mate was slightly unhinged.

He was also a bit worried that the ridiculous contraption on her head did nothing to dim her bright light or his attraction to her.

"Come on, Tarek. We have no idea what to expect

here and it would be best if the humans didn't catch sight of our ears. Just put it on, okay?" She tried to shove the hat back at him.

It might be black as opposed to white, but it was still fuzzy. Worse, it too had eyes and ears and to his horror, an actual snout. "What exactly is it?"

"It's a black bear. I thought you would prefer it to the bunny rabbit, but we can switch if you like."

"I don't like. You need to think of something else because I'm not wearing the severed head of any animal."

"It's not—oh, fine!" Luna waved a hand over the bear and the threads disintegrated and transformed, creating some other strange looking hat-thing.

"It still has eyes."

"They're not eyes. They're goggles. It's an aviator hat."

Tarek shook his head. "What does that mean?"

"Pilots used to wear them, but now I guess they're quite popular among the general population."

Tarek scowled. He had no idea what a pilot was and he wasn't thrilled at the idea of covering his ears, but it was definitely an improvement over the bear. "Are the goggles really necessary?"

"I suppose not. They do complete the look, though."

He let out a groan. "Fine. Just give it to me."

She smiled and handed it over.

He turned it in his hands, then settled it on his head. "There. Satisfied?"

She tilted her head and stared at him a moment, then stepped forward, reached up and adjusted the hat carefully.

As she did so, her fingers brushed the tip of his left ear.

Even through the thick fabric, he felt that touch to his very core and barely managed to restrain the feral Fae inside who roared, "Mine!"

They stood there for a long moment, staring into each others' eyes, then Luna stepped back.

"The sun is rising," Tarek murmured. "Shall we greet the dawning of the day?"

She nodded, peeking up at him from beneath that ridiculous bunny-rabbit head, then grabbed his hand in hers and led him to the edge of the canyon.

Standing there, side by side, hand-in-hand, neither spoke as the world came to life around them, the sun slowly rising over the vast canyon of the tribes, painting its walls and the sky above in brilliant shades of orange and red.

CHAPTER 2

$\mathcal{I}$N FAERIE, LUNA had a network of spies available to her at all times.

Faerie itself whispered to her—the lands rolling beneath her feet, the trees sending messages with the rustling of their leaves, the flowers building a path to show where she needed to go.

It was this network of spies that had made it possible for her to track the roaming Veil in the first place.

With Faerie always showing her the way, the one thing Luna feared the most about this trip to the mortal side of the Veil was the very likely chance she'd be cut off from the natural world.

She wasn't sure Tarek had noticed the subtle ways Faerie changed in Luna's presence. When she'd been younger, the flowers and butterflies had followed her everywhere, her magic so strong, it had spilled over constantly until she'd finally learned the art of containment.

Her magic still overflowed—it was too strong and too connected to the natural world to do anything else —but it did so in more subtle ways now, flowers springing up in her periphery rather than directly where she stood and butterflies flitting and landing nearby rather than on her form.

Luna's visits to the mortal side of the Veil in the past had revealed a land that had fallen mostly silent. She'd often felt cut off from the natural world there, especially when they visited the areas the mortals called cities.

However, there were some spaces she'd visited in the past that felt like tiny pockets of Faerie. The vast canyons of the Tribes had been one of those spaces.

However, as the world brightened around her, Luna realized even the canyons were fading now.

This land was in pain.

She could feel the scars upon the earth where mortals had mined resources without enough care for the physical world, somehow in the process poisoning the earth in ways they probably didn't even understand.

It broke Luna's heart.

Her magic responded to the pain and surged from

her in a vast wave, burrowing deep into the lands of the tribes and spreading far and wide.

She thought about calling it back, thinking perhaps she shouldn't interfere, but restraining her magic in the presence of such pain would only cause more suffering, both to her and the lands around her.

"What did you do?"

Of course, Tarek had sensed the surge in magic.

"The lands are suffering. My magic could do no less than respond."

"It's traveling too far. You need to call it back."

Luna smiled. "It doesn't work that way. It's disconnected from me now and has a life of its own. Magic lives in these lands now, the way that it lives in Faerie. It will travel and grow and heal the scars of this earth wherever it finds them."

"You gave away your magic?" He asked incredulously.

"Of course not. The magic isn't finite. It's infinite in the way the sky is infinite, in the way that life is infinite. The magic will multiply as it travels and perhaps will even find a few worthy mortals along the way."

"By the fates! You've unleashed wild Faerie magic on the mortal side of the Veils? What were you thinking?"

Luna had no answer, for the truth was the magic had responded to the need it sensed and there'd been no stopping it, but she wasn't about to admit that to

Tarek. She feared he would view her as flawed, the way many of the Fae did, believing her unable to control her gifts simply because they misunderstood the nature of earth magic.

Fae trained for years to gain affinity with the different gifts of Faerie, to wield the magic of air, fire and water, of earth and life.

The latter two were the most difficult to command as they were the most feral of all the Fae magics.

As such, no one controlled them, though many believed they did.

Earth magic responded to the needs of the land and healed and bloomed and grew wherever it wished.

The Fae were simply a vessel to house that magic for short periods of time before unleashing it upon the world.

It was simply good fortune that most of the time, the Fae's will and the will of the magic were the same.

In Luna's case, though, earth and life magic were inextricably entwined, and as such, were so feral, her parents had insisted she hide her gifts as much as she could while growing up, for such wild magics were rarely seen outside the Royal line.

Of course, hiding her magic was not something Luna had excelled at, so instead, she'd pretended she had no control over it, acting flighty and carefree, which had led to many judgmental looks over the years.

What no one—not even the most blessed in gifts of the Fae—seemed to understand was that her magic was so much a part of her, it lived on her skin, breathed when she breathed and acted on her thoughts before she even knew they'd formed.

Luna was as much a part of the natural world as any Fae born had ever been.

As a result, she'd worried about being trapped on mortal land, afraid it would not communicate with her in the same way that Faerie did.

In truth, she'd worried these lands were dead.

They'd been dying the last time she'd visited and she'd wanted to unleash her magic then, but she'd been with her family and they had helped her contain the wild and untrained magic that had strained for release.

"Seriously, Luna. What were you thinking? If a mortal somehow gains access to the magic—"

"Don't be ridiculous. It is of Faerie, a magical blend of earth and life, and it will not be vulnerable to corruption." She refused to think of how her parents would disapprove or of how Mitaru would give her that look of disappointment. Her brother was one of the missing now and her parents were long gone and this land needed her magic in a way it hadn't even a hundred years before. She turned away from the canyon to look toward the path leading up. "We should go now. I sense mortals approaching."

At that moment, a young man and woman turned the corner at the top of the path and walked down it toward them.

"Good morning!" The woman said cheerfully as she passed Luna and Tarek.

"Good morning," they replied as the man walked by with a nod.

The woman and man didn't pause at the overlook where Luna and Tarek had watched the sun rise, but instead continued along the walkway, heading down toward the canyon below.

"I suppose we should go up, then," Tarek said.

"We're not far from the top. I'm actually pretty impressed, to be honest. The Veil could have delivered us at the very bottom of the canyon. That would have left us facing an extraordinarily long hike."

Tarek let out a snort. "It could have delivered us mid-air atop the canyon and let us freefall to our deaths." He scooped an arm around her waist and murmured, "Good thing I'm an expert in air magic." With a small pop of said magic, he sent them from the ledge where they'd been standing to the top of the path where the woman and man had first appeared.

"Tarek!" Luna gasped, horrified at the risk he'd taken, though also thrilled to find herself in his arms once more. "You can't do that. What if a mortal had seen?"

"If you can send your earth magic traveling through the lands of this world without even a tether to pull it back, I can certainly use a bit of air magic to save us some steps. Now let's figure out where we are and how to get to Lawrence, Kansas."

An hour later, they stood inside what the mortals called a Visitors Center.

Luna was happily chatting with mortals about who knew what, but Tarek was too lost in shock to pay any attention.

He hadn't believed the mortal realm could be that different from Faerie. After all, he'd been there once before—a thousand years back or so—and it had seemed much the same.

Lands as far as the eye could see.

Apparently, a thousand mortal years was enough time to change everything, though.

There were dragons in this world!

And they traveled on things called wheels and were made of steel and other unnatural things.

Luna had laughed when he'd exclaimed, "Dragons!" and had called them cars and trucks and SUVs, whatever that stood for. She'd admonished him for not doing his homework, for not learning as much as he could about the mortal world before latching on and hitchhiking—there was that word again—his way across the Veil.

As far as he was concerned, though, it didn't matter what they were called.

They were clearly evil. One had squawked a terrible sound as it almost ran him down.

Tarek had reached for his sword, only to realize it had been left behind, which made no sense considering he'd had it on him when entering the Veil.

He'd barely restrained his shouts when Luna had admitted the roaming Veil had probably stripped him of it. "They're unpredictable," she'd reminded him. "Just be happy it didn't steal your arm or something else you'd be missing a whole lot more."

"That was a possibility?" He'd exclaimed in horror. "That I might lose an arm?"

She'd shrugged. "Or a leg, possibly an eye. They're not to be trusted. A roaming Veil is not the same as the Veil you serve as a Guardian, Tarek. You should know this."

"Unpredictable, yes, but amputation was never mentioned as a possibility."

"And this is why you shouldn't have latched on. I wasn't prepared for a hitchhiker, you know. Losing your sword was really the absolute best you could hope for."

Considering the best meant his weapon of choice wasn't with him in a land he didn't know, Tarek hadn't been pleased.

He'd followed her into the Visitors Center, grumbling the entire way, worried he'd be fighting dragons without a sword for as long as it took them to find their way to Kansas and possibly even for the rest of his life because he wasn't about to travel back to Faerie through another one of those roaming Veils.

He scowled at Luna.

She really should have told him the risks! It was quite rude actually, to drag him along without informing him he might arrive without his limbs.

Never mind that she hadn't wanted his company.

She still should have informed him!

This was why, as she was chatting with mortals, making friends for some unknown reason, he was obsessing over the fact that he could be standing there armless or possibly not standing at all because his legs had been lopped off.

Irresponsible and completely reckless.

He'd wager even Zara hadn't realized how risky this endeavor was.

If she did realize it, then that meant she'd left him in

the dark as well, which would give him a reason to yell at both sisters.

"I've discovered there's something called the Internet—they didn't have that the last time I was here—and it's apparently a source of endless information and will tell us anything we want, including how far away Lawrence, Kansas is," Luna informed him after finishing her conversation with the mortals and skipping back to his side. "I wasn't sure how to access this internet, so a woman looked on some weird black box thingy and told me it's approximately twelve hundred miles away."

"Twelve hundred—" Tarek was so horrified, he couldn't even get out the final words. "Even with my air magic, it will take us a ridiculous amount of time to travel that far. We'll be on the road for at least a month."

"Don't be ridiculous. We're not going to walk to Kansas."

"Well, thank the fates. I assume you found us some horses, then?"

Luna snickered. "Of course not. We'll take the bus or maybe a train."

"And what exactly are those?"

"Lamest road trip ever!" A young female mortal with bright purple hair stamped past them, a mutinous look on her face, before whirling to glare at another female mortal who was following close behind.

This second female was older, but looked enough like the youngling—though without the purple hair—that Tarek assumed they had to be related, possibly mother and daughter.

"I thought you would adore this trip, darling. I chose it specifically with you in mind. After all, you used to talk about the fairies incessantly."

"Yeah, when I was five. But these are not fairies, Mom. There's not a thing about them that resembles Tinkerbell."

"What's a Tinkerbell?" Tarek muttered to Luna, who shrugged in response.

"Well, no, I suppose not, but—"

"Not to mention the fact that I had a life back in California, one that I quite enjoyed, thank you very much. I was looking forward to hanging out with my friends this summer and instead, you're dragging me halfway across the country—"

"Friends?" A boy-child scoffed as he approached with an adult male at his side. "As if you have friends."

"Oh, shut up, you dweeb monster."

"All right, that's enough out of both of you," the woman said.

"Can't we just go home now? Bad enough I've had to climb all over this lame canyon, but the camper is entirely too small with Bobby along." She glared at the boy Tarek assumed was probably her younger brother.

"It wouldn't be too small if it weren't filled with all your beauty supplies." Bobby lifted his fingers and wiggled them and down while saying the word beauty.

"What do you think that finger motion signifies?" Luna whispered.

Tarek shook his head. "No idea."

"Please, Mom?" The young girl pleaded. "We've been gone a week and I've missed so much already."

"That's enough, Madison," the man said. "This is a family vacation and we won't be cutting it short. We've got quite a ways to go until we've reached our destination, which means you'll probably be miserable the entire way if you can't find something positive to focus on."

"We're headed for Kansas," Madison sneered. "What could possibly be positive about that? There's nothing worthwhile in Kansas."

"Of course, there is," Bobby said, then began to tick them on with his fingers. "Toto, twine, tornadoes, just to name a few."

"What's a Toto?" Tarek muttered, somehow riveted by the scene playing out before them.

"I don't know," Luna whispered back, "but they're going to Kansas, which is great news for us."

"Twine?" Madison repeated in an incredulous voice.

Tarek had to agree. He couldn't understand what

the appeal of rope would be. Though perhaps it had some other meaning in the mortal world.

"Sure, I read all about it in the travel guide," Bobby said. "We can—"

"Not interested," Madison said, lifting her hand and shoving it into his face.

For a moment, Tarek was certain she was going to hit her brother, but the palm of her hand stopped a mere centimeter from his nose.

"Rude!" Bobby snarled, jerking away.

"As I said, that's plenty out of both of you," the man said. "It's time to get on the road, so make your pit stops and let's get going."

"Fine." Madison stamped off, Bobby following in her wake.

"Well, come on," Luna said in a rather loud voice as she led the way closer to the mortal couple. "We need to figure out how we're going to get to Lawrence, Kansas."

"You're heading to Lawrence?" The woman asked.

"Oh." Luna did an excellent job, Tarek noted, of appearing both surprised and innocent, as if she hadn't deliberately moved closer to ensure the other couple would hear her. "Yes, we're very excited to visit the Fae." Sincerity rang through her voice. "My name is Luna Evaria and this is my husband, Tarek."

Tarek jolted a little when she used his last name and then again, when she claimed him for her husband, though he supposed it made sense. They were mates, after all.

"It's very nice to meet you," the woman said with a smile. "We're the Winters. I'm Mary and this is Rob. Our children are using the facilities, but they should be back soon. We're also headed for Lawrence. I'm hoping we can meet the Fae, especially the princesses."

"Oh, yes, that would be wonderful," Luna agreed. "We were just trying to decide how we were going to get there. I don't suppose you would have a recommendation? We were considering the bus or perhaps the train, but as we've never made this trip before, we're not quite certain which would be best."

"Well—" Mary hesitated and glanced toward Rob, who simply shrugged in response. "We've been traveling by RV and it's really wonderful because we can stop whenever we want and make little side trips to see the most interesting of places. The RV has plenty of room if the two of you would like to join us."

Luna glanced over at Tarek, a look of uncertainty on her face.

He stepped forward and caught her hand in his, then realized she'd snared him with her glamour.

By the fates, she was good at projecting a mix of innocence with just a touch of fear.

"I don't know," she murmured. "That would be amazing, but are you sure we wouldn't be a bother?"

"Of course not," the woman exclaimed, a look of joy on her face. "We'd be delighted."

Tarek had no idea why she was so happy, other than that he was pretty certain Luna was to blame. Whatever magic she was weaving, it was both subtle and powerful.

Then the two children returned.

"What's going on?" Madison asked suspiciously.

"We've made some friends, darling," Mary gushed. "This is Luna and Tarek. They'll be joining us for the rest of our journey."

"Are you serious?" Madison exclaimed. "As if the camper isn't small enough, now we're adding two more people?"

"Hush now, Madison," Mary admonished. "We've got plenty of space and these two are in need of a ride. Luna, Tarek, these are our children, Madison and Bobby."

"Hello," Luna said with a smile.

"Hi!" Bobby grinned at her. "Do you like to play games?"

"Well, I haven't had much practice, so you'd probably have to teach me, but I would be delighted to learn."

"Sweet!" He crowed and quickly latched onto her hand. "I have lots of games. You're going to love them all."

Madison let out a snort of derision.

"Right then, now that introductions have been taken care of, it's time for us to hit the road." Rob clapped his hands and headed for the door of the center, calling over his shoulder, "Follow me, troops."

A short walk later, Tarek was horrified to discover that an RV was just another word for steel dragon. Worse, it was the largest specimen he'd seen to date.

He wanted to balk, but Luna didn't hesitate to follow Mary and Rob as they led the way up some steps into the RV. Of course, Tarek could not allow his mate to take such a risk on her own, so he followed her into the belly of the beast.

Madison and Bobby followed behind him, Madison glaring the entire way.

"They're not going to take my bunk, are they?" she demanded the moment they arrived inside.

"What do you think?" Mary glared at her daughter, who let out a huff.

"Well, I don't see why I have to give up my bunk. They could take Bobby's instead."

"Because they're married and your bunk is larger, so you'll be getting your things and moving to the other bunk in Bobby's area."

"Oh, that's not necessary," Luna began, but Rob cut her off.

"It absolutely is. Madison needs to learn manners

and how to be gracious." He gave his daughter a pointed look.

She scowled and stamped off.

"I'm gonna get us set up to play games, Luna!" Bobby exclaimed.

"Three board games first," Mary insisted.

"*Mom*, board games are boring."

"Then play a card game instead. With *real* cards."

"Fine." Bobby stamped off as well.

"Right, we're off then. Make yourselves at home." Rob headed toward the front where he settled in a seat there and started the dragon with a rumble.

Tarek shuddered. This was not how he'd envisioned this journey going.

"All right, Bobby, Madison," Mary called out, "time to buckle up."

"Mom, I'm getting the games," Bobby called from where his head was buried in a cabinet at the back of the RV.

"Just take what you've got to the table and get buckled in." She turned to Luna and Tarek. "I'll give you the quick tour, shall I?" She then proceeded to walk them through the inside of the RV, showing them first a small table and 2 booths she called the dinette, a couch across from the dinette that she waved at and referred to as the living room, a small kitchenette, a small closet-like space that hid two bunk beds, one on top of the other—Madison glared down at them from the top bunk when her mother opened the door and was admonished to get down and into a seat with a belt immediately—a bathroom and another bedroom at the back of the RV.

"This is our bedroom," Mary said to them. "Feel free to escape in here if the children are bothering you. Your bed is at the front above the cab. I'll show you how to set it up once we stop for the night. In the meantime, help yourselves to whatever you need. I'll be up front with Rob." With that, she left them alone.

Tarek waited until he was sure she was out of earshot before asking, "How in all of Faerie did you get her to invite us along on this journey?"

Luna gave a tiny shrug and a smile. "It's called charm, Tarek. You should attempt to find some."

"I'll show you charm," he growled, sliding an arm around her waist and capturing her lips with his.

CHAPTER 3

ONE MINUTE LUNA was teasing Tarek, and the next, she was inundated with heat as he dragged her into his arms and kissed her.

She lost all train of thought, clutched his shirt and kissed him back.

Long moments slid by, one by one, as she fell into a world where nothing else existed but Tarek and the desperate need that barreled through her.

"Luna," he murmured against her lips, sending shivers down her spine.

She wrapped her arms around his shoulders and strained closer.

They might have stood there forever, drowning in the passion of their first kiss, had Bobby not called out, "Luna, I'm ready for our first game!"

A few moments later, Luna was sitting at the dining room table across from Bobby with Tarek at her side. "All right, we're here. So what are we playing?"

"War."

"War?" Luna glanced at Tarek, who gave a tiny shrug. "Exactly how old are you, Bobby?"

"I'll be ten next month." He grinned proudly.

"Oh, dear. I'm not sure about this. After all, a card game named War sounds a bit violent. Perhaps we should check with your mother first."

Bobby let out a series of rolling chuckles, his eyes bright with amusement. "It's a card game. It's not violent!"

"Are you sure because with a name like war—"

"I'm sure." Bobby's chuckles were infectious and Luna couldn't help but giggle with him.

"Very well, then. Why don't you explain to us the rules?"

Bobby nodded enthusiastically and starting talking super fast as he divided the cards among the three of them.

"Hold on. Did you just say the king is worth more than the queen?"

"Of course," Bobby said.

Tarek snickered.

"But that's not right," Luna exclaimed. "The queen

should be worth more or at the very least equal to the king."

"Nah," Bobby said. "No one ever plays that way."

"Well, I don't see why not."

"I agree." Madison, who had been pointedly ignoring them up to this point, stood from where she'd been reading on the couch and joined them at the table. "Go ahead and deal me in, but we're playing queens high."

"But that's not in the rules," Bobby protested.

"New rules," Madison said. "Deal me in."

"Fine. I have to start all over again now." He gathered the cards back up, then shoved them at Madison. "You shuffle this time."

Madison rolled her eyes, but began an interesting and complicated process of separating and then mixing the cards back together.

"You're quite good at that," Tarek said.

Madison shrugged and quickly divided the cards among the four of them.

What followed was a bit of chaos as they each "battled" for ownership of the cards. After the first game, which Bobby won, Madison insisted they shuffle in a second deck, which meant the second game took quite a bit longer, but was even more chaotic than the first.

"War!" Bobby crowed, making Tarek groan and Madison and Luna giggle.

What followed was an epic battle as the two somehow managed to turn over the same card three times in a row.

Luna was completely enchanted by Tarek's ease as he teased Bobby about what had clearly become the challenge of a lifetime.

"Third time should have been a charm." Tarek scowled at his cards.

"Not for you it wasn't!" Bobby chortled in joy.

"Hmmm." Tarek looked at Bobby suspiciously. "Where'd you pull that queen from anyway?"

"I had it all along!"

"Well, you've been lucky so far, but you're going down now, Bobby, my friend," Tarek said, laughter in his voice.

"No way, man." Bobby bounced in his chair, practically vibrating with excitement. "I'm king of this battle and you will bow down before me."

"We'll see about that," Tarek said. "On three. One–two–"

"Three!" The four of them chorused as Bobby and Tarek turned over their 16th battle card and 17th of the round.

"Yes!" Bobby crowded, raising his fists high in the air, clearly delighted at the Ace he'd just turned over to beat Tarek's pathetic two. "I am the champion! I am the champion!"

Luna and Tarek laughed while Madison just rolled her eyes.

Luna could tell from the expression on Madison's face, though, that she was thoroughly enjoying Bobby's antics.

Bobby gathered his cards together and in the next couple rounds, knocked Tarek out of the game, then Luna and then it came down to just him and his sister.

Madison teased that she was going to beat him right up until the very end when he won her final card.

She giggled and ruffled his hair. "Don't let it go to your head, dweeb monster."

"Pit stop," Rob called from the front seat as he turned into what looked to be another parking lot.

A pit stop, Luna discovered over the next few hours, meant many different things.

Sometimes it meant they were stopping for fuel for the RV. During those stops, it was also an opportunity to use public restrooms instead of the one on the RV, to stretch their legs, and to fetch drinks and snacks.

Luna also discovered there were such things as "boring" snacks and "road-worthy" ones. Apparently, fruit and cheese were the former, while crunchy things that turned one's fingers red and set one's mouth on fire were the latter.

Tarek and Luna agreed—they preferred boring snacks.

Still, it was fun at each pit stop, to listen to the kids' opinions and test the many options they deemed roadworthy.

So far, Luna had tried something called candy rocks that zipped around, popping in her mouth, tiny round cookies with little chips of chocolate, triangular crunchy things called Doritos (she preferred the Cool Ranch favor) and something called Oreos.

By the time Bobby had properly instructed her on how to eat an Oreo (so many steps), Luna was feeling rather ill.

"What was in that food?" she groaned.

Tarek chuckled. "I told you to stick with cheese and fruit."

"Oh, don't worry," Madison said cheerfully. "You're just transitioning from the sugar rush to the sugar crash."

"Sugar rush?" Tarek asked.

"Sugar crash?" Luna didn't like the sound of that.

"Pit stop!" Rob called out.

Luna groaned. She couldn't possibly eat another morsel. When she informed Rob and Mary of that, they both grinned.

"Oh, this is a different kind of pit stop," Mary said with a happy smile.

"Oh, no," Madison groaned.

"Great," Bobby said morosely.

"What are we visiting today?" Madison asked. "Is it the last bite of a chocolate bar someone failed to eat?"

"Nah, that's too last year," Bobby said. "I bet it's the largest doo-doo someone's pet dinosaur made."

"Gross," Madison said.

"Doo-doo?" Luna asked.

"Poop," Bobby said cheerfully.

Luna grimaced. "Sorry I asked."

"All right, you two. That's quite enough," Mary said. "I'm sure you're going to love this stop. It's been recommended over two thousand times on the Trailer Mamas group chat."

Madison groaned. "Seriously? You're taking recommendations from people who call themselves Trailer Mamas?"

"I don't see what's wrong with the name. They live in trailers, they're mamas, seems perfectly legitimate to me."

"You're hopeless," Madison said.

"Well, come on, then," Rob said. He'd exited the vehicle from up front and had walked around and now stood staring up at them, waiting for them to disembark.

"Must we?" Madison asked.

"Yes," Mary said. "You must." She leaned forward and murmured in her daughter's ear. "And your father's been looking forward to this stop, so try to be nice."

"Fine."

A few moments later, Luna and Tarek stood beneath a huge sign that announced they were entering the "Gardens of Rubbish," and stared in disbelief at the sheer volume of stuff in front of them.

Luna took a giant step back to look up at the sign again.

Yep. It said exactly what she thought she'd read.

"Isn't rubbish another word for trash?" Tarek asked.

"I think so," Luna said, "and based on what we're seeing, I'd say that's accurate. What's not accurate is using the word *garden* to describe this place." Earth magic practically vibrated inside her, wanting to be released to show these mortals what a garden *should* look like.

"I thought Rob said this was a pit stop," Tarek said.

"Oh, it is," Madison said as she passed them by. "It's a stop where we gape at roadside attractions that are typically the pits."

"Interesting," Tarek muttered. "Well, come on then. We might as well get it over with." Grabbing Luna's hand, he pulled her forward and onto the path—the only part of the area where the ground was visible.

As they walked down the path, Luna marveled at the piles of *stuff* that surrounded them for as far as the eye could see.

A few moments later, they found Mary standing in front of a very large container of some sort.

"What is it?" Luna asked.

"It's a vase?" Mary said it like a question. "Maybe? I'm honestly not sure." She beckoned them closer and whispered, "The owner told me his mother made it, so I'm not going to ask what it's supposed to be." She stared at it a beat longer. "I'm also not going to buy it, but I thought I should stand here for a moment or two and appear as if I were at least contemplating it."

"Very thoughtful of you," Luna said, "but I think you've pondered it enough, don't you?"

"Definitely." Mary chuckled. "Let's go see what the kids have managed to find. I'm sure it won't be anything good."

They wandered further down the path, Tarek behind them.

To the left were more strange creations that Luna now presumed were also made by the owner's mother. There were giant, hollow containers next to incredibly tiny ones.

They were all in strange shapes, lopsided or top-heavy or somehow asymmetrical in a way that disturbed the eye. They weren't painted, but rather covered in small pieces of a strange substance that Luna couldn't quite identify at first glance.

"I've figured it out." Mary came to a stop next to a

towering vase-like structure that stood taller than Tarek and wider than the trunk of a tree.

"You have?" Luna asked.

"I think they're eggshells."

"Mom! Mom!" Bobby came dashing up. "You're still in the first garden."

"There are more?" Mary asked faintly.

"Yeah, this is just the first one. There's a garden of chairs and a garden of silverware and even a garden of toilets!" He let out a shout of laughter. "I counted ten of those, then I came to find you. You have to come and see!"

He led them through the rest of what Luna assumed was the garden of containers, then through a garden of bicycles (all of which appeared to be missing at least one, if not both, tires) followed by a garden of chairs (which appeared to be mostly broken), through a garden of tools where Rob was happily wandering, and finally to the infamous garden of toilets, where Luna was pleased—and a bit disturbed—to discover that it somewhat resembled an actual garden.

A pathetic one, but a garden nonetheless.

Every single one of the toilets was filled with potting soil and from that soil bloomed a few straggly plants.

Luna didn't even realize her magic was being called

until it was too late and the toilets started to shudder a bit.

"Oops," she whispered to Tarek.

"What do you mean oops?"

"We should maybe hurry them along."

He glanced around, then let out a sigh. "Just couldn't resist, could you?"

She shrugged. "It's the way my magic works."

Luckily the path didn't wind back on itself, which meant that Mary and Bobby were moving forward, and therefore, didn't see when the plants all around Luna and Tarek burst from the soil, overflowed the toilets and ran across the path.

"Moving along," Luna said, grabbing Tarek's hand and dragging him after Mary and Bobby.

In the end, they spent close to two hours in the Gardens of Rubbish.

Much to everyone's surprise, the only one who actually bought something was Madison who, in the Garden of Signs, had found two she declared she couldn't live without.

Madison had just paid for her signs when a customer staggered down the path, dragging a three-wheeled wagon behind him.

Inside that wagon was a toilet overflowing with purple flowers.

"Never seen your toilets bloom like this before,

Bucky," he said as he dragged his find to the register. "Looks like you've finally developed a green thumb. My mama's gonna love this addition to her front yard."

"Huh," Mary said as they headed back toward the RV. "I must have missed that toilet. All the ones I saw had dying weeds in them."

"Sorry, Mom," Bobby said. "It must have been hidden in the back because I didn't see it either."

"Oh, that's okay, darling. It would have taken up too much space in here anyway." She followed Rob up the steps and disappeared into the RV.

Bobby skipped back to Luna and declared, "This pit stop wasn't as bad as some others we've been on."

"True," Madison agreed as she came up beside them. "I wouldn't count on them all being as interesting as this one though. In fact, I guarantee there's much worse to come." With that, she climbed into the RV, Bobby on her heels.

Luna glanced up at Tarek, who just grinned. "If this is interesting and there's actually worse to come." He shook his head. "I'm flat-out speechless."

Once back on the RV, they discovered Mary was making everyone sandwiches called grilled cheese. Luna had believed she couldn't possibly eat another thing, but the minute she smelled those sandwiches, she was ravenous.

The kids sat at the dining room table while the

adults hung out on the chairs and sofa in the living room and enjoyed the meal together, talking and laughing.

It was nice feeling part of a family again.

Luna missed her brother and meals like this, from the early years when their parents had still been alive to the later years when it was just Mitaru, Zara and her.

Once Mitaru crossed to the mortal world and was trapped there, though, meals were never quite the same.

Tarek reached for her hand and squeezed it gently, offering comfort without her even asking.

This was what it was like to have a mate. Someone who knew when she was hurting, who knew when she needed comfort, who would always be there for her no matter what.

Strange how she'd gone from loathing the sight of him to craving him, all within the span of a single day.

"Excellent lunch, Mary. That really hit the spot." Rob stood and rubbed his hands together.

"It really was," Luna said. "I've never had a grilled cheese before and now I realized I've been terribly deprived."

Mary chuckled. "Well, it's easy enough to fix, so I'm guessing you'll never be deprived again."

"So we have probably another hour before we reach our destination for the evening," Rob said. "Everyone get settled and buckled up. We'll be leaving shortly."

Bobby immediately tried to convince Mary to let them play his video game—whatever that was—but Mary reminded him he needed to play a third board game or card game before he could move on to video games.

Bobby let out a huge sigh, then brought out a card game he called *Exploding Kittens*.

"Are all the games violent in this realm?" Tarek whispered in Luna's ear.

"I certainly hope not," she whispered back, "but I'm beginning to wonder."

As Bobby started to explain the rules of the game (with many interruptions from Madison, who was pretending to read a book, but was clearly more interested in what they were up to than in the story), Luna found herself asking repeatedly, "But *why* do the kittens explode?"

Tarek clearly found her confusion to be hilarious because he kept snickering under his breath as Madison and Bobby attempted to explain.

Unfortunately, neither one had what Luna considered to be an adequate reason for such a violent result.

"Just go with it," Bobby finally said.

"Yeah," Madison agreed. "It's supposed to be funny."

"But they're kittens. Those are baby cats, right?"

"Yeah," Bobby said.

"So how can that be funny? Exploding innocent kittens?"

"They don't *really* explode," Bobby said. "It's just pretend, Luna."

Tarek snickered again and she thrust her elbow into his side.

He just grunted, then lifted her wrist and placed a kiss in the palm of her hand.

Bobby made a gagging sound, then demanded, "Are we ready to play yet?"

Luna really wanted to ask what the point of the game was, if the explosions were just pretend, but she could tell Bobby was impatient to start playing, so she simply nodded and said, "I think so."

Bobby started dealing out the cards, and Madison joined them, having decided her book just wasn't that interesting.

As the game progressed and kittens were exploded —or not exploded in some cases—Luna continued to obsess over the same questions she'd had in the very beginning.

Why did the kittens explode, *why* would anyone want to explode them in the first place and *why* did Bobby and Madison seem to think it was hilarious?

There really were no answers to those questions and after one game that thankfully didn't last too terribly long, Luna was extremely gratified to hear Bobby announce that it was time to play his video game instead.

She still had no idea what a video game was, but she was certain it couldn't possibly be sillier or more distressing than a game involving kittens exploding everywhere.

Tarek couldn't think of the last time he'd been so amused.

Luna's reaction to the kittens was hilarious and the kids' attempts to explain why the explosions were supposed to be funny rather than upsetting made the entire situation even funnier.

Of course, he happened to agree with Luna that the title of the game was unnecessarily violent, especially when it was directed at such innocent creatures, but he wasn't going to admit that.

Not when it was so much fun to watch her grimace in disgust every time someone turned over an exploding kitten card or slump in relief when they managed to block that horror.

It was quite possibly the most entertaining half hour of his life to date.

He couldn't wait to tell Thorne all about the game and Luna's reactions.

His smile faded as he thought of his brother.

By the fates, he hoped to have the opportunity to tell Thorne this story and others.

Luna leaned her head against his shoulder, offering comfort without him saying a word.

Tarek dipped his chin to the side and placed a kiss on top of her head.

Bobby made another gagging sound, then announced loudly, "I hereby declare this area a no-kissing, no lovey-dovey, no hanky-panky zone."

Mary gasped and swiveled around in her chair at the front of the RV. "Where did you hear that?"

"Hear what?" Bobby looked confused.

"*Hanky–panky*. Do you even know what that means?"

"'Course I do. It means kissing and gross stuff like that, which is why this whole RV is now a love-free zone."

"Well, I have some bad news for you, Bud," Rob called from the driver's seat. "Your mother and I are very much in love and there *will* be hanky-panky later tonight."

"Rob!" Mary gasped even as Bobby let out a dramatic groan and Madison squealed, "Ew, gross, Dad."

Luna giggled and Tarek's shoulders shook as he tried to contain his laughter. "Guess you're out of luck, Bobby."

"Bummer," Bobby muttered.

"All right, fam," Rob called out. "We've arrived at our campgrounds for the night."

The next hour was spent getting "hooked up," which was a process Tarek found to be completely fascinating. Power and water and sewer were all managed through hoses and cords.

It was truly ingenious.

In fact, the evening was full of wonders that kept Tarek in a constant state of amazement.

After the RV was completely hooked up, Rob enlisted Tarek's help in setting up an outside area as well.

With the push of a button, an awning extended from one side of the RV and created a covered porch. Rob then pulled out some lawn furniture that was somehow stored beneath the RV.

Tarek wondered if the mortals were so incredibly innovative simply because their lives were so short.

Perhaps they made so many discoveries in such a short time because they were living their lives on fast forward.

Many thousands of human lives would past by in a tiny fraction of a Fae's.

Perhaps this too was why in some ways, the Fae often made changes so slowly, they seemed to be standing still. When you had enough time to achieve everything, the passage of time really had no meaning at all.

The Fae could undoubtedly learn quite a bit from the mortals' sense of urgency.

The evening passed swiftly. They had something Rob called a cookout with hamburgers and hot dogs (the latter of which Tarek found to be disgusting) and the adults sat around laughing and talking while the kids sat in front of the TV in the motorhome playing video games.

Their laughter spilled out into the night and filled Tarek with a sense of contentment.

When Mary eventually announced she and Rob were retiring for the evening, Tarek found himself amazed once again, this time because she showed him how the space above the driver's cabin could be transformed into another bed.

She unhooked a ladder from a ledge above the driver's seat, hooked it to a couple straps, then climbed up and showed Tarek how to finish off the sleeping space.

He was still marveling at the ingeniousness of the space when she bid him goodnight and headed toward the back of the motorhome.

Luna stepped up beside him. "That's a really small space," she observed. "I guess I didn't exactly think things through when I introduced us as husband and wife. I just figured they'd be more accepting of us if they believed we were married."

"We're mates. It's much the same thing," Tarek said.

"Except we haven't exactly had a ceremony yet, so we're more like engaged, rather than married."

He grinned at her. "Engaged or married, it matters not, my love, for we were meant to be."

CHAPTER 4

THE NEXT SEVERAL days were amazing.

They traveled a couple hundred miles every other day, with frequent pit stops, sometimes for snacks and sometimes for what Madison called, "ridiculous roadside attractions."

Like the Monster Wax Museum somewhere in New Mexico that made Madison roll her eyes and Bobby bounce with joy.

They took something called selfies there—images that made Luna wince when she saw them, for in every single one, she looked like she needed rescuing from the monster standing in the background.

"They're not really selfies if you don't take them yourself, you know," Bobby informed her.

"I didn't know that," Luna said. "So what are they then?"

"They're just photos."

"Nobody asked your opinion, Bobby," Madison snapped. "Luna, you need to get closer to Tarek. Tarek, you need to look like you're going to fight that blood-sucking demon."

Luna shot a look over her shoulder at the very pale wax figure standing behind her. "He's a demon?"

"He sucks blood?" Tarek demanded at the same time.

"He's a vampire," Bobby said. "Of course, he sucks blood."

Luna shivered. "Like the cochari."

"Yeah, except they look like us," Tarek muttered. "With rounded ears, of course. Do you think these demons actually live here in the mortal realm?"

"I sincerely hope not."

"Perfect!" Madison exclaimed. "Good job looking completely freaked out, Luna."

"That's because I *am* freaked out," Luna said. "This place is creepy."

It just got worse from there. The monsters got scarier, Bobby got more and more excited to act out increasingly terrifying scenes and Mary and Rob just looked on indulgently as Luna was made to play the damsel in distress over and over again as Bobby and Tarek rushed in to save the day.

"These are the best pictures ever," Madison announced at the end of the day. "I'm totally posting them on social media."

Luna had no idea what that meant. She was just happy to escape the terrifying museum.

There were other roadside attractions, of course.

Rob and Mary made the last-minute decision to travel north to Colorado rather than continuing East toward Texas, which was how they ended up spending hours in a dinosaur-gnome garden in a small town along the border of Colorado and Arizona.

Then, still in Colorado, but mere yards from the Kansas border, they ended up spending an entire day attending a paintball festival where visitors were given canvas bags full of paintballs that they threw at each other.

It was an insane day of fun as everyone ran around the outdoor arena, trying not to get hit with paint, but inevitably being covered in it.

After each day of travel, they stayed at the campsite for an entire day and evening, which gave Luna the opportunity to try and communicate with the lands.

She and Tarek went for long walks and on those walks, her magic broke free again and again, seeping deep into the earth to travel far and wide.

As the days passed, each day of travel followed by a day attempting to heal the lands, Luna grew paler and weaker.

The only relief from the unrelenting pain was the laughter she found when playing games with the children and the peace she felt each night when she slept in Tarek's arms.

As the days went by and her energy levels dipped further and further, Tarek grew more and more concerned.

He tried to convince her to take a break, to stop communing with the lands. "At least stop until we reach Lawrence. Then, if we need to, we'll come back and try again, but we'll bring more Fae with us so you're not trying to do it all alone."

"I just can't, Tarek. The lands are dying and I cannot ignore their suffering."

"Even though it means you're suffering instead?"

She shrugged. "My suffering is nothing compared to what they're going through. The lands are screaming in agony and I can help them, so I simply must. Please try to understand."

He sighed and kissed her. "I thought you said the magic disconnected from you, that it worked independently from you, so why is it draining you so very much?"

"I don't really know how to explain it. Yes, it disconnects from me and yes, when it does, it becomes its own entity, independent of my needs or desires. However, each time the magic breaks away, it takes a bit of time for me to regain my energy, and since I'm no longer able to draw energy from Faerie, since we're no longer connected, it just takes me longer to recover. It's an unsolvable problem really. As long as these lands are weak, I cannot recover as quickly as I should, but so long as I do not recover, these lands cannot become strong or at least not as quickly as I'd like."

Tarek let out a rumble of displeasure, then said, "Fine, but I reserve the right to carry you back to the motorhome if I sense you floundering."

"Deal."

When they returned to the motorhome, they found Rob and Mary waiting for them.

"We don't usually like to drive at night," Mary said, "but we think we should go ahead and travel across the border into Kansas. We think you might feel better, Luna, once we're inside the Fae shield."

Luna jerked. "Why—why would you think that?"

"What Fae shield?" Tarek asked at the same moment.

"We won't say anything, so please don't worry. It's just, well—"

"It's pretty obvious you're not from around here," Rob said. "Add in the hats you never take off, hats that completely hide your ears from view, and we're pretty certain we've been helping a couple Fae make their way home."

Luna blinked back tears. "Yes. I'm sorry we deceived you, we just weren't certain—"

"Please don't apologize," Mary said gently. "It's been an honor traveling with you both, but now we're concerned. It's become clear to us both that you're struggling, Luna. You've lost weight, you're pale. We're close enough to the shield, we should have just continued on, rather than stopping for the festival."

"Oh, no. The children had such a wonderful time," Luna said, "and so did I."

"As did I," Tarek said.

"I will always cherish the memory of traveling with your family and especially of the day we spent laughing and tossing paint at each other." She glanced up at Tarek, who nodded. "We will never forget any of you."

Mary nodded. "Let's get you back to your people then, shall we?"

Luna smiled. "Oh, yes, please."

Thirty minutes later, they crossed the border from Colorado to Kansas and about ten minutes after that, they went through an invisible barrier that was immediately recognizable as a construct of Faerie.

"It feels like we just passed through the Veil." Luna could already breathe easier and the air felt lighter and cleaner. "It's almost as if we've entered Faerie herself."

She could no longer hear the land screaming in agony, and hope filled her heart once more.

"The lands," she whispered to Tarek. "They're healed here."

A look of joy crossed his face. "There must be other Fae working to heal these lands as well. If you decide we need to venture out again, there will be other gifted Fae to help with the effort."

"It's the princesses," Mary said.

"Astra and Glory?" Luna asked.

Mary nodded. "Princess Astra has a gift for healing the lands. Well, all of the Fae do, really." She got an arrested look on her face. "I just assumed—you've seen your website, haven't you?"

"What's a website?" Luna asked.

"Oh, my goodness."

"Here." Madison appeared beside the couch where Luna and Tarek were sitting and handed Luna her tablet.

Luna just stared at it.

While she might have learned what it was called simply because Madison was on it constantly, she certainly had no idea how to use it.

"Madison, what are you doing up?" Mary asked in exasperation.

"You seriously think we wouldn't notice when the engine started up and the RV starting moving?"

"Yeah, Mom, it was totally obvious something was up." Bobby walked into the living room.

"How much did you hear?" Luna asked.

"You mean about you being Fae?" Bobby grinned. "Because we already knew about that."

"Yeah, it was kind of obvious," Madison said.

"Especially after you made those toilet plants grow at the Rubbish place," Bobby said. "That was totally cool."

"Wait, you guys knew way back then?"

"Well, not immediately," Mary said, "but when we got back to the RV that day, there really was no hiding it."

"Have you never looked in the mirror after using a lot of magic?" Rob called back from the driver's seat.

"Oh no," Luna groaned. "My eyes."

Tarek chuckled. "I can't believe we didn't think about your eyes."

"The whites completely disappear," Bobby exclaimed. "It's totally cool!"

"It's a genetic anomaly," Luna said. "I don't know anyone else who has this problem, except for my sister, Zara. And it's definitely *not* cool when you're trying to travel incognito. I was totally Unveiled to you guys this entire time."

"Well, think of it this way," Tarek said. "At least we've managed to stay Veiled when in public so far, which is a pretty big accomplishment. I should point out, though, that we would have remained Veiled with the Winters as well, if you'd *just* resisted the urge to use your magic."

Luna scowled at him and he chuckled again.

"I still can't believe you've known all along," Luna said to Mary.

"Well, even if we hadn't learned after you made the toilet plants grow, these last few days would have given it away."

"What do you mean?" Luna glanced at Tarek, but he just shrugged.

"Oh come on," Rob called back. "Did you seriously think Mary and I wouldn't notice that you two would go out for a walk, then suddenly be in bed without the door to the RV even opening?"

Luna sent Tarek a look, but he just shrugged. "Hey, if I can't use my air magic to transport my mate to bed when she's exhausted from healing mortal lands, then I have no idea what it's good for."

"In other words, I wasn't the *only* one having diffi-culty resisting the urge to use my magic."

Madison giggled.

"So I guess I can finally take this stupid hat off," Tarek said and promptly pulled the aviator hat off his head.

"Oh, but it was so cute on you," Mary said.

"Yeah, and I've gotten rather fond of my hats," Luna said. "I especially love this one." She pulled the pink hat from her head. "What did you call it again, Madison?"

"A caticorn."

"Caticorn. I think I would like to meet a caticorn one day."

Bobby snickered.

"Unfortunately, no one's ever met one." Madison grinned. "I'm pretty sure someone just made it up."

"What does that mean?" Luna asked.

"Invented it. Like, it's not a real animal."

"Oh. Well, that would be a shame," Luna said.

Tarek just grinned.

"All right, Madison, Bobby, since you're both already up, I'm not going to make you go back to bed," Mary said. "But you do need to sit down and buckle up."

Madison rolled her eyes. "Fine, but first—" She leaned over and touched the screen of her tablet. It came to life and Luna's breath caught because staring out at her from the screen was Princess Astra.

"Just press that little triangle there." Madison pointed to a white triangle at the bottom of the screen. "Once you do that, it'll start playing."

"Playing what?"

"The video. Go ahead."

Over the next hour, as Rob drove them toward a

new camping ground inside the Fae shield, Tarek and Luna stayed riveted to the tablet, watching video after video of Princess Astra and her Royal Guard as they traveled across the territories they'd claimed for the Fae, healing the lands and talking with mortals and Fae alike.

Luna cried as she listened to stories from so many Fae, who were heartbroken to be cut off from their homes and their families.

Then, there came a video that made her heart stop and had Tarek making a sound as if he'd taken a punch to the torso.

"Thorne," he said, his voice broken.

"Kalina," Luna whispered.

There on the screen, Thorne and his mate Kalina rode horses, flying the banner of Faerie between then, leading endless lines of Guardians through a fading fog, across a bridge.

"Where's Mitaru?" Luna whispered. "He's always at Kalina's side. Where is he?" She blinked back tears as she scanned the rows of Guardians, seeking just one glimpse of her brother.

But he wasn't there.

A single tear broke free.

He wasn't there.

Not in the first unit that marched free of the mist and not in the second.

He wasn't in the third or the fourth or the fifth units.

But then there he was.

Astride a huge black horse, dressed all in black, he rode at the side of Princess Glory.

Luna burst into tears, so grateful to see her brother for the first time in over three years that she could barely breathe through the joy and the pain.

Tarek lifted her onto his lap, then wrapped his arms around her, set his chin on her hair and squeezed her tight.

Together they watched both their brothers—one at the start of the long lines of Fae, and one at the very end—ride across the screen in proud formation, and as they watched, they both wept tears of joy and relief.

"**A**stra!"

Astra jumped at the sound of her name being roared by her mate.

By the fates, he could be loud when he wanted.

She had no idea why he was yelling though. After all, she hadn't done anything to aggravate him lately.

Not that she remembered anyway.

Kalina had sent someone for him a few moments

before, which probably meant whatever she'd had to tell him was *not* good news.

"We had a deal!" He stormed into the conference room where she was meeting with her sister, Glory, and both their Royal Guards.

Kalina, Thorne and several other Guardians followed him in.

"What deal is that?"

"That you wouldn't sneak out to heal the lands without me."

"And I haven't."

"Then how do you explain this?" He whirled and swiped a hand across the wall. Their Fae browser appeared, along with a number of icons.

He tapped one Astra recognized as a national news network, then waited.

As soon as the page finished loading, he began swiping through several videos at the top until one popped up that said, "Will the Fae claim the Grand Canyon next?"

Astra slowly rose to her feet, peripherally aware that Glory had risen as well to stand at her side.

Kahji hit play, then stepped back so he stood on Astra's other side as the news report began.

"We're standing here at the site of one of hundreds of uranium mining claims that surround the Grand Canyon," a newswoman announced on screen.

"According to locals and environmental experts, these mines represent a significant danger to the entire Grand Canyon region, exposing the watershed and wildlife to toxic chemicals and other pollutants.

"Many of the uranium sites have been abandoned over time, but proper clean-up wasn't always undertaken, which means that most sites, whether currently active or not, continue to represent a potential source of pollution.

"Beginning about a week ago, however, the land itself appeared to be fighting back."

The picture cut to what was clearly an amateur video taken on a cell phone.

Green vines began to climb giant metal scaffolding, making it shudder and creek.

More and more vines crawled across the land, disappearing into a giant hole in the ground.

Dirt began to pour into the hole and the scaffolding began to slowly tumble to the earth, the vines wrapped around it somehow slowing its descent.

Foliage rushed across the ground, covering the metal so that it disappeared under a blanket of green, appearing to be nothing more than a part of the natural earth within a few moments.

"That wasn't me, Kahji," Astra said.

"You're sure?"

"Of course I'm sure. The Grand Canyon is more

than a thousand miles from here. There's no way my magic has traveled that far and I assure you I haven't broken our deal."

"It wasn't me either," Glory said, probably in response to Kahji sending a questioning look her way. "And I'm not sure I know of any other Fae with enough power to accomplish what we just saw, certainly not at that pace, at least not without help."

"I do, though there's no way she's here on the mortal side of the Veils."

Astra turned to look at Mitaru, one of the Guardians of the Western Veil, but before she could ask for more information, the newswoman was back, claiming their attention.

"What you see here—" The woman turned slightly and gestured toward the forest behind her. "—is a site, much like the one in the video, that has been overtaken by the natural world around it, in this case the Kaibab National Forest.

"You cannot really tell at this point, but a week ago, this entire area was surrounded by a chain link fence. It was also the site of flooding ever since the mining company managing it hit groundwater.

"Unfortunately, the waters that regularly erupted from this site were contaminated. This has caused much worry for the local tribes and residents who feared the source of their drinking water might be next.

"It appears, however, that their worries may now be over, for there is no evidence of the contaminated waters that once flooded this area nor even of the mine shaft once drilled here.

"We're told that this scene has played itself out over and over again at hundreds of mining sites that dot the lands surrounding the Grand Canyon, with each of those sites now looking as if they are part of the surrounding landscape, no evidence of mining in sight.

"Perhaps even more interesting than these extraordinary events, is the fact that we've also been told that there have been no Fae sightings at all in these areas, which leads us to wonder: has the environmental work of the Fae begun to spread beyond the lands they've claimed or are there more Fae walking among us than we realize?

"And finally, perhaps the most important question of all: what lands will the Fae come for next? Perhaps the Grand Canyon itself?"

"Great, just what we need," Glory groaned. "More ammunition for the mortals to hate us."

Astra shrugged. "I'm not concerned about the mortals. Whoever it is out there, healing the lands, good for them. They need healing. I'm just worried we have a vulnerable Fae who hasn't managed to make it home to us yet."

She glanced around the room. "Has anyone heard rumors of more lost Fae?"

When everyone answered in the negative, she looked at Mitaru. "Who is it you think might be out there?"

Mitaru shook his head. "I don't see how it could be her. She wasn't traveling here when the Veils closed and though she's extraordinarily powerful, I don't think she could have done this from Faerie."

"Who, Mitaru?"

"My sister, Luna."

CHAPTER 5

LUNA'S ENERGY WAS back with a vengeance the following day and she had a fabulous time playing board games, card games and video games with Bobby and Madison.

She especially enjoyed playing *Bio Fae*, a video game that had been created by the Fae themselves.

"It's to raise awareness of their efforts to save the earth," Bobby informed her.

"It's amazing." She couldn't believe how crisp the scenery was and how much the little people they called avatars resembled Fae she actually knew.

She could pretend to be one of the princesses or their mates, one of whom was her brother, Mitaru!

She could pretend to be a Guardian of the Veil, like

her friend Kalina, who also happened to be Mitaru's best friend and commander.

She could even pretend to be a mortal working alongside the Fae, doing what she could to help them heal the planet.

"I really wanted Fae Warfare," Bobby said, "but that was before I met you and Tarek."

"Fae Warfare? That one's not made by the Fae, right?"

"Nah, it was made by mortals and Mom told me the Fae are trying to save the earth, so it wouldn't be right to fight them or even to pretend to.

"At first I was annoyed, but now that I've met you guys, I guess I don't mind so much. Besides, this game is pretty cool, even though I've only managed to plant one forest and clean up one river."

"That's pretty amazing, though."

"Yeah, but the river keeps getting contaminated again because it's connected to all these other rivers that I haven't cleaned yet, so it's a lot of work, constantly cleaning the same river."

Luna nodded. This must be why she kept getting drained. No matter how much magic she sent out, it was never enough because the land was so huge and all of it interconnected.

"Plus there are evil people constantly getting in the way of my progress. Every time I destroy a factory and clean the river, the corporations just build another one and it's always bigger. Then there are the people from the government. They want to arrest me so I'm constantly on the run from them."

"Really?"

"Yeah. They say the Fae are thieves for stealing the land and giving it back to the indigenous peoples."

"Indigenous—you mean the tribes?"

"Well, yeah."

"Why do the lands have to be given back? We Fae left the lands to the tribes when we retreated millennia ago."

"Exactly!" Mary exclaimed. "That's what Princess Astra said. We didn't know that history, you see. We didn't know the Fae existed at all, but then Princess Astra explained the land belongs to no one and that the indigenous tribes are just its caretakers."

"Of course, the government doesn't like that explanation," Madison said.

"Neither do the corporations," Bobby said.

Of course, then he'd had to explain what a corporation was, which had led to many other discussions, but in the end, Luna was convinced this was why the Veils had closed.

"The land's been dying for generations," she murmured that night to Tarek while they lay in bed, arms wrapped around each other.

"I know, my love. I can feel it too."

"It's terribly disturbing." She fell silent for a moment, then started speaking again. "I think this is why the Veils closed. We're needed here, Tarek, the Fae are, to beat back the dark, to care for these lands once more."

"I just hope we don't pay the price like we did long ago."

"I think that's why Princess Astra constructed the shields." Luna thought back to the reports and videos she'd watched of those shields being formed, then expanded to envelop more and more lands. "I wonder if she understands what she's built here. A Judicia forest and three shields on mortal lands, at least one of those shields as close to an actual Veil as I've ever felt? She's created a mini Faerie right here in the mortal world, a place of sanctuary for all of the Fae and a transitional passage that could theoretically stand as a gateway between Faerie and the mortal realm, a changeover passage if you will, with the true Veil to Faerie at its center."

"I hadn't thought of it that way," Tarek said. "But you're right. The lands she's claimed do a pretty good job of surrounding the city she's chosen, though there are some gaps."

"Yes." Luna tried to picture the altered map of the United States and the Fae shield that surrounded territories at its center. There were gaps on the Eastern side, in the north and in the south. "She needs to claim part of what the mortals call Iowa and Arkansas, then we need to heal the lands she claims. Once that has happened, it's entirely possible the Veil to Faerie will open once more."

"We'll be able to share your theory with her soon enough. Now sleep, my love, for there is nothing more you can do for these lands tonight."

The next several days of travel were wonderful.

Now that she was feeling so much better, Luna insisted that Mary and Rob not alter their travel plans any more than they already had.

It hadn't taken much video-watching to realize they had altered their course to avoid Texas for reasons that had nothing to do with their desire to visit Colorado instead.

The government of Texas had declared any Fae found within their borders was subject to immediate execution and had authorized ordinary citizens to execute them.

Many mortals had been accused of being Fae and shot by their neighbors as a result.

Though lawsuits had been filed and the federal government itself had issued a cease and desist to the Texas government, the law condemning the Fae had not been repealed.

In fact, there were many articles online speculating that Texas was on the verge of seceding from the United States, though many other articles insisted it wasn't possible.

Luna found the entire concept of borders and states and countries to be both fascinating and ludicrous at the same time. The mortals were one people with one earth, one home to call their own, yet they would divide themselves and call themselves other, destroy their earth in their pursuit of power and something they called money, and ultimately destroy everything they worked so hard for.

It simply defied reason or logic.

"I've decided it's because we live such short lives," Rob explained one evening when she asked the question as delicately as she knew how. "When you only have a hundred years to live—more likely, less than that —you feel like you have to *have* everything, *know* everything, *be* everything as quickly as possible because it all could be gone tomorrow."

In a truly horrible, tragic way, that made complete

sense.

It also made Luna even more determined not to deny these mortals the vacation they had planned and so she insisted no side trip, no pit stop, and no roadside attraction was to be skipped.

This was how she ended up taking some truly ridiculous selfies with Tarek and the Winters as they traveled across the state of Kansas.

First, they visited a hand-dug well that boasted it was the largest in the world.

Tarek wondered how they could possibly know such a thing. Had all hand-dug wells in this world been measured?

Madison took a picture of them giggling under the sign for the preposterously named roadside museum, "World's largest collection of world's smallest version of world's largest things."

While it was fun to actually visit the collection, especially when they recognized miniatures of actual large things they'd visited on their road trip, all of them agreed afterward, it was the sign with the ridiculous title that made the trip worthwhile.

At that point, they were way off course, so they just continued to meander through small Kansan towns, visiting whatever took their fancy, including the twine Bobby had mentioned days earlier.

"It really is just a ball of rope," Tarek muttered. "Sure

it's the *biggest* one I've ever seen, but I'm still not sure I see the appeal."

"It's huge!" Bobby crowed as he raced under the structure where the twine sat, ginormous and fat, and leaned up against it.

He spread his arms wide and grinned at Madison. "Take my picture, Maddy!"

"All right, all right, hold your horses."

"What do you think would happen if it started to roll away?" Bobby demanded after giving his approval to the pictures Madison had taken.

"I think it would take the force of a thousand Fae to make that thing move," Tarek said, "but if it did, well, I imagine it would smash pretty much everything in its path."

"Yeah," Bobby said. He ran around to the side of the giant ball, leaned into it with his hands and made a fierce face. "Everybody watch out. I'm about unleash my mighty ball of twine and you'll be squashed flat! Splat!"

"Hold that pose," Madison called. "And push as hard as you can."

Bobby strained forward, but of course, not even a single strand moved.

Tarek grinned. "Should I—"

"Don't even think about it," Luna said.

He chuckled while Bobby and Madison consulted over her phone and the photos she'd taken.

Of course, that wasn't the end of the picture-taking.

Mary and Rob got their own photo taken, then they had one with the kids, then Madison made Tarek, who had the longest arms, take a selfie of all six of them, then she took a picture of Tarek and Luna together.

It was Luna's favorite picture so far.

Tarek stood behind her, arms around her waist, and she was leaning to the side a bit and looking up over her shoulder.

He was looking down at her and they were both laughing.

It was one single moment that Madison managed to catch in all its perfection.

After the twine, they visited an enormous toilet bowl that Bobby found to be hilarious. It had water inside it and a long rope that when you pulled actually flushed the water and refilled the basin.

Bobby, of course, had to flush it several times.

Their last stop of the trip was in a town called Abilene where they visited a giant spur, something the mortals wore on their cowboy boots to spur their horses forward.

Luna and Tarek were both horrified at the concept, but that didn't stop them from joining the Winters in trying on cowboy hats at the western store the spur towered over.

In the end, they each bought a cowboy hat and exited the store with the hat on their heads.

For Luna and Tarek, this was the first time they'd bared their Fae ears in public and it caused a bit of a stir.

Families thronged to them and asked to take selfies with them in their cowboy hats, so a second round of photos were taken under the Big Spur once more, first with Madison and Bobby ("Because we get the first photos with your ears on display, that's only fair," Madison insisted), then with all six of the Winters and finally with the many families waiting patiently in line.

Of course, the process delayed them, but eventually they pulled out of the parking lot, waving goodbye as they went.

"Just a hundred and fifteen miles to go," Rob announced. "Problem is daylight is waning and these highways out here are pitch black. What do you say we find one final campground, then head out in the morning?"

Of course, everyone agreed, and so it was, with both joy and a bittersweet sadness, that Luna and Tarek spent their final evening with the Winters family at a campground about ninety miles west of Lawrence, Kansas.

They stayed up late, playing games, talking and laughing, before they finally retired to their beds, unable to stay up any longer.

The next morning, Luna and Tarek stepped outside just as the sky was beginning to lighten and, as they'd done every day for the past thirteen, sat on the RV's steps to watch the sun rise.

"Still no word?" Astra asked.

"There are rumors, of course," Talvenia, captain of Glory's Guard, said.

"What kind of rumors?" Glory asked.

"Well, there's this town newspaper in Arizona that reported toilet bowl plants growing at an unprecedented rate."

"*Toilet bowl plants?*" Kahji asked incredulously. "What in the world are those?"

"Plants actually grow in toilets here?" Dyranel, a member of Astra's Royal Guard, looked confused. "Because that would be weird, wouldn't it?"

"Very weird," Lumina, another member of Astra's Royal Guard, said.

"Seriously, who wants plants in a toilet?" Dyranel asked.

"Not even the mortals could want such a thing," Nako, one of the Guardians of the Veil said. "Could they?"

"All right, enough," Astra said. "I think we can assume that if there is a Fae out there, they would not be making plants grow in toilets, so let's move on, shall we? Any other rumors or sightings?"

"No, but I have a report from a Colorado border town," Mitaru said.

"The Kansas border?" Nako asked.

"No, Arizona."

"Interesting. I have one from a Colorado town along the Kansas border."

"All right, let's hear them," Glory said impatiently.

"I'm not sure I understand the reporting," Mitaru said. "The people keep talking about gnomes and dinosaurs."

"Aren't dinosaurs extinct?" Dyranel asked.

"They are, but apparently there's a garden in this town full of fake dinosaurs and gnome-creatures."

"What are gnomes?"

"Never mind the gnomes. What did you hear?" Glory asked.

"The garden grew overnight to such proportions all the gnomes and dinosaurs are hidden from view."

"Well, gnomes aren't very big," Nako said.

Everyone stared at him.

"What? I looked it up." He pointed at the surface of the table in front of him where a picture of a gnome had appeared.

"Ugly little thing," Talvenia, who was seated next to him, said.

"*Anyway*," Mitaru said, "the dinosaurs *are* quite big and they've disappeared as well. Considering the growth happened overnight, it might be worth a look."

Astra nodded. "What did you hear about the town on the Kansas border, Nako?"

"Apparently a paintball festival had some issues due to trees suddenly showing up on their route, when no trees had been there when the planning occurred."

"What's paintball?" Talvenia asked.

"It's a shooting game humans play," Mitaru reported.

"I doubt a Fae would participate in a shooting game," Astra said.

"This particular festival doesn't involve guns," Nako said. "Apparently participants *throw* the paintballs instead."

"Okay, so those are possibilities. Any other rumors we should check out?"

At that moment, a knock came at the door.

"Enter," Astra called.

"My apologies, Princess Astra and Princess Glory." Yiveren, a member of Kalina's unit of Guardians, stepped inside. "There are reports of two Fae in

Abilene. Photos of them posing with mortals are trending on social media. I don't recognize the female, but I met the male at Kalina and Thorne's mating ceremony.

"Thorne, I believe it's your brother, Tarek."

CHAPTER 6

THE FINAL DAY of traveling was spent much the way previous traveling days were. Everyone got up early and had breakfast together.

The adults then worked together to unhook the RV and pack everything away, then they were off.

As they traveled the final ninety miles toward Lawrence, the kids, Luna and Tarek played endless rounds of War, much like they had that first day together.

"We've got company," Rob called out an hour into their journey.

"What kind of company?" Luna asked.

"The Fae kind." Mary threw a huge smile over her shoulder at them.

"Really?" Bobby scrambled to open the shade beside

them.

As far as the eye could see, Guardians on horseback stood on the grassy plains that ran alongside the highway.

As they passed each horse, its rider wheeled the horse around and rode behind the line of Fae, keeping pace with the RV.

Within minutes, the number of Fae riding at their side increased until even the sound of the wheels on the highway were drowned out by the thudding of the horses' hooves.

"Are they going to ride beside us all the way to Lawrence?" Madison asked.

"It's an honor guard," Tarek said, "come to escort us home."

Thirty minutes later, they reached the exit for the city of Lawrence and passed through a secondary shield.

The Fae who had traveled with them split into two groups, half leading the way down the exit into town, the other half falling in behind their RV.

As they circled the entrance to enter town, they found themselves facing a wall of trees at the bottom of the ramp.

"The Judicia forest," Luna whispered, slipping free from the booth to walk toward the front of the RV. "I can't *believe* how powerful Astra is."

"I can't believe how powerful you are," Tarek murmured in her ear as he came up behind her. "My beautiful, talented, *gifted* mate."

The many Fae riding before them did not hesitate in the face of so many trees, but simply rode at a steady pace toward the forest, which parted to let them through.

"Just follow the Fae, Rob," Luna said as he let up on the gas.

"That pathway looks really narrow."

"It will widen for us. Trust me."

"All right. Here goes nothing."

He drove slowly into the forest and just as Luna had promised, the road widened, trees shifting back to allow them safe passage.

"That's so cool," Bobby breathed behind them. "Did you see the trees moving?"

"I did," Madison said. "I can't believe we're actually *inside* the secondary shield."

"I know," Bobby exclaimed. "My friends said we'd be lucky to get past the first one."

Luna squeezed Tarek's hand, then headed back to the dinette, where she slid into the booth again. "The shields allow passage or not based on your intent, Bobby. If you'd approached the shield wanting to hurt someone behind it, you would never make it through. You're a good person, though, as are your parents and your sister, and you're all friends to the Fae. As such, you would never be denied entrance."

"Did you hear that, Madison? We're friends of the Fae!"

"I know."

Tarek joined them and they all settled back to watch the forest as it shifted around them, trees sliding in and out of position as needed.

Fifteen minutes later, they finally exited the Judicia forest and entered the town of Lawrence, which was like no other town they'd seen on their trip so far.

The streets were not paved the way the rest of the roads they'd traveled had been paved. Instead, they were made of cobblestone and rumbled beneath the RV's wheels, making for a bumpier ride through town.

The buildings were all covered in foliage and there were gardens literally everywhere, on top of buildings, in between them, dripping over rooftops and spilling down the sides of buildings, filling abandoned cars, creeping across cobblestone streets, winding around lampposts and mailboxes.

"I've never seen anything so beautiful," Madison said.

"I haven't either, honey," Mary called from the front. "I'd heard that Lawrence, Kansas was one of the most beautiful sites on earth, but I didn't expect this."

"I think we're approaching another shield," Luna said. "This one feels even more powerful than the last."

Tarek gave her a startled look. "Really? I can't feel anything at—" He broke off just as there came a yank on Luna's magic. She barely caught the reins in time.

"Wow, that's *powerful.*"

"I should learn not to doubt you." Tarek shook his head. "I didn't feel a thing until we went through it."

"I think that's the way it's supposed to work."

"It's a castle," Madison exclaimed, for once sounding as young and as excited as her brother, but Luna and Tarek had seen who was waiting in the courtyard of that castle and were already moving.

Rob had barely stopped the RV before Luna was shoving open the door and leaping down, Tarek seconds behind her.

"Mitaru!"

"Luna!"

She flew into her brother's arms and held on tight. Long moments passed before he pulled back.

"Zara's fine," she said quickly. "She was supposed to come with me, but she got called to the Royal palace unexpectedly and I couldn't wait for her because I might not get another chance!"

"Thorne!" Tarek raced to his brother, who flung his arms around him and hugged him tight.

"Tarek." Thorne's voice was choked with emotion.

A long moment later, the brothers separated and Tarek was treated to hugs from Nako, Thorne's best friend who was like another older brother to Tarek, and Kalina, Thorne's mate.

"I cannot believe I'm here with you right now," Tarek said.

"*How* are you here with us?" Thorne demanded.

"Did you resign your commission as a Guardian of the Veil or did they grant you leave?" Nako asked. "Or are you on a mission for the Guardians?"

Tarek shook his head. "No to all of those questions. A friend begged me for help, worried because her sister was about to jump through an unstable, roaming Veil in an attempt to find her brother, and she was planning to do it all by herself."

"He'd better not be talking about you, Luna," Mitaru growled.

Tarek grinned. "Sorry to have to tell you this, Mitaru, but Zara was the friend, so yes, it was Luna she demanded I save."

"I didn't *need* saving, thank you very much." Luna glared at him.

Tarek grinned. "True. She would have done fine without me, though perhaps not considering she managed to send us to the top of the Canyon of the Tribes."

"I would never have been in danger of falling off in the first place if it weren't for you."

"Hold up," Mitaru snapped.

Tarek could tell Mitaru wanted to glare at his sister, but since she was still plastered to him, cheek pressed to his chest, arms clutching him tight, he apparently decided to settle for glaring at Tarek instead, which didn't exactly seem fair, but whatever.

"Did you just say you almost fell *off* the Grand Canyon?"

"Is that what the mortals are calling it these days? And no, I didn't almost fall. I almost *stepped* off it because I was annoyed at Tarek, so really it's all his fault."

Mitaru's glare intensified. A moment of silence passed, then he exclaimed, "Wait a minute. You two have been traveling *alone*, together?"

Luna jerked away from Mitaru, set her hands on her hips and glared at him. "Don't you take that tone with me, especially when I happen to know that you were traveling across country with your mate before the mating ceremony as well. Congratulations, by the way."

"Yes, well, she was my mate *and* we were accompanied by five full Guardian units, not to mention her Royal Guard."

"Well, *we* were accompanied by the Winters family." Luna turned and waved at the Winters, who had opened up the awning on their RV and were all sitting in their lawn furniture, eating from bowls of popcorn and watching the show.

Tarek snickered at the sight.

"Also," Luna said, "it just so happens that Tarek is my mate."

"Really?" Thorne exclaimed at Tarek's side. "You found your mate?"

Tarek nodded. "I did."

"Congratulations, brother. I'm so happy for you." Thorne slung his arm around Tarek's shoulders and grinned at Luna. "Welcome to our family, little sister."

Luna beamed back at them. "Thanks! We waited to have the mating ceremony until we could celebrate with our brothers."

Mitaru scowled. "You mean to tell me I just got my baby sister back and she's already being stolen from me?"

"Aw." Luna whirled and hugged her brother again. "I'm so happy to see you, Mitaru. So happy." She sniffed and hid her face in his chest.

He wrapped his arms around her and dropped a kiss on her head. "I feel the same, Luna. You've made me incredibly happy." He drew in a deep breath, then held out his arm to Tarek. "Welcome to our crazy family, Tarek, brother of Thorne."

Tarek grinned and clasped his arm tight in a warrior's hold. "My thanks, Mitaru."

*L*una was still crying a little when Mitaru turned with her in his arms so that she faced the princesses.

Luna gasped.

How had she missed them standing *right there?*

She hadn't even acknowledged them, had just run to her brother, hugged him, then lectured him, then cried all over him.

Thank goodness they were both smiling at her, not seeming at all perturbed at her behavior.

"Princess—princesses. I don't know who to address first." She giggled.

"Well, normally, I would say Astra since she's the oldest," Princess Glory said, "but since Mitaru is my mate, that means you and I are going to be like sisters, so I think you should choose *me* first." She smiled. "Fair?"

Luna giggled. "Perfectly fair. It's so nice to meet

both of you and I'm so happy to know that you both have found your mates, and am happier still to know that one of them is my brother."

"It's nice to meet you too, Luna," Princess Astra said. "We cannot wait to hear the story of how you managed to make this journey, but all of that can wait until after your ceremony and celebration."

"Fae," Princess Glory shouted. "We have another mating ceremony to celebrate!"

Cheers erupted from all sides and while the Fae shouted out congratulations, Glory stepped closer to Luna and murmured, "Let's get you ready, shall we?"

"Yes, that would be wonderful. Oh, but—can Mary and Madison come? They've been with me this entire time and I wouldn't feel right leaving them out of the preparations."

Glory looked over to where the Winters were sitting, eating popcorn and talking, then said, "What about the boy and his father?"

Luna glanced over her shoulder at Tarek. "Rob and Bobby are with you," she called to him. "I'm taking Mary and Madison with me, got it?"

Tarek grinned. "Got it, mate."

Luna faced the RV where all four Winters were staring at her with stunned looks on their faces. "Well, come on then, Madison and Mary. Time to prepare for a genuine Fae mating ceremony."

Madison let out a whoop of joy and leapt to her feet, dragging her mother with her.

That was how Luna ended up walking across the Fae courtyard into their castle on the mortal side of the Veils, with two Fae princesses and two mortals at her side.

*H*ours later, the sun was slowly sinking in the sky when Luna met Tarek by a lake that stood not far from the Fae castle and, with their brothers, the Winter family and hundreds of Fae and mortals in attendance, exchanged vows with him.

"Luna." Tarek held her hands in his and stared into her eyes. "I see eternity in your eyes and no matter the length of our days, I shall know peace so long as you are by my side. I offer you everything that I am, everything that I have been and everything I've yet to become, in this realm and in any other, in this lifetime and in all the rest. With you, for you, I am my best self."

Though she was far from Faerie and though her best friend and sister, Zara, was not in attendance, Luna had never felt so blessed as she was in that moment, listening to her mate pledge himself to her.

It was with true joy in her heart that she offered

hers back to him. "Tarek, my love. I see eternity in your eyes and no matter the length of our days, I shall know peace so long as you are by my side. I offer you everything that I am, everything that I have been and everything I've yet to become, in this realm and in any other, in this lifetime and in all the rest. With you, for you, Tarek, I am my best self."

"A thousand blessings be upon this mating." Princess Glory was the one who spoke the traditional Fae blessing before slamming her hands together and sliding one palm over the top of the other, flinging magic of the Royal line across the space between them.

Her magic rained down upon Luna and Tarek, sparking and sizzling everywhere it landed, making the blood in their veins boil with power and their mate bond throb with joy.

Luna was leaning toward Tarek, love and hope overflowing her heart, when Fae witnesses leapt forward and swept them apart.

As was tradition, the mating celebration that followed was filled with joy and dancing and music that lasted the night through.

As was also tradition, the Fae did an extraordinary job of keeping Tarek and Luna far from each for most of the night, though they did occasionally allow them together on the dance floor, for a quick kiss before swooping them away again.

Once Bobby caught onto what was happening, he took great joy in running interference, darting forward and asking Luna for a dance or dragging Tarek away just as the two of them were about to reach each other on the dance floor.

His laughter filled the space and made everyone around him, Fae and mortal alike, smile in reaction.

Thorne and Mitaru also enjoyed running interference, each of them dancing with Luna while their mates danced with Tarek, then spinning Luna into Tarek's arms for a brief moment, before spinning her away again.

Even Rob and Mary got into the spirit of things, pulling the two apart right when they ended up facing each other on the dance floor.

As Rob swept Luna away, he told her that Princess Glory had invited them to make their home there in Lawrence, among the Fae.

Luna beamed. "And? Will you stay?"

"I put it to the vote with the family and much to my shock and amazement, it was unanimous in favor of Kansas. Even Maddy voted yes."

"That's quite the miracle right there." Luna giggled.

"It's because of you and Tarek. You've opened our eyes and our hearts and have shown us everything that we have to be grateful for. We're looking forward to seeing what the Fae will accomplish for humanity and hopefully to being part of that process." With that, he spun her into his daughter's arms, who giggled and grabbed hold of Luna's waist and led her into a spirited dance full of spins and hops and slides.

Eventually, Madison danced Luna into the arms of Tarek, who solemnly said, "You were always my favorite, Madison," making her giggle and rush away as Tarek pulled Luna into his arms and kissed her.

Heat built and Luna thought she might melt right there on the dance floor, but then Bobby was there, exclaiming, "I said no hanky-panky!" which had all the Fae within hearing distance (which was most of them) hooting with laughter.

"Yeah, no *hanky-panky,* Tarek." Thorne laughed, then stole Luna from Tarek's arms and passed her into Bobby's. "Take her away now, Bobby. She's not to be dancing with her mate anytime soon."

"Aye-aye, captain!" Bobby grabbed Luna's hands and took off with her, galloping in giant circles around the dance floor. "Did you hear, Luna? We're going to stay here in Kansas with you!"

She beamed at him. "I heard and I'm so very happy. It's the best news ever."

"I know, right?"

It truly was a magical evening, filled with family and friends and laughter and joy.

It was also filled with a bit of torture as the heat

built between Luna and Tarek, their longing for each other growing as the night progressed.

Each time their hands met for a brief caress or their lips for the occasional passionate kiss, only to be pulled apart once more, the intensity of their desire grew.

Finally, in the wee hours of the morning, Tarek and Luna managed to sneak away from the celebration.

They ran hand-in-hand down the hill toward the castle and sneaked inside to the quarters they'd been given, where they lunged into each other's arms and kissed.

Luna clutched at Tarek's tunic, dragging it from his form, then rubbed against him, trying desperately to get closer.

She kicked off her slippers while he pulled the tie that held her dress together at her left shoulder.

The dress fell to the floor in a swish of fabric and she was in his arms again.

He kissed her voraciously and still kissing her, stumbled toward the bed with her in his arms.

He lay her upon it, then followed her down, settling over her form, pressing her deep into the bed and making her heart race with desire.

"Tarek," she whispered as he threaded his fingers through her hair and stared into her eyes.

Luna, my love.

Tears formed as she heard his voice for the first time

in her head. *Tarek, my one true mate, my love.* She wrapped her legs and arms around him and lunging upward, captured his lips with hers.

He rolled them across the bed, kissing and caressing, long moments lost as the heat between them built to unbearable degrees.

She rose above him, adjusted, then sank down upon him, slowly taking him deep.

They both groaned, then he surged up and rolled them so she was on her back staring up into his eyes once more.

My Luna. He began to move, slowly drawing back, then pressing forward, making everything flutter as he did so.

Tarek. Oh, by the fates. Tarek.

He moved faster and faster until she could barely breathe through the heat and wonder.

All Luna knew, all she could feel was Tarek, both inside and out, everywhere. He was her everything.

Luna, my love.

Tarek! She flung her head back, eyes blind as the world shattered around her.

arek gasped for breath as he lay upon their mating bed, his gorgeous mate at his side. "I believe you have destroyed me, my love. You may have to leave me here forever."

Luna giggled, then rolled so she was sprawled across him. She settled her arms on his chest, then her chin on her hands and beamed at him. "When I made this crazy plan to cross the Veil, I thought Zara would be the one to accompany me. Then, when she was called away just as I'd tracked down the Veil once more, I had this terrible feeling inside that this would be the moment I actually found it, *because* she wasn't with me.

"I tried to convince myself it was unlikely I'd find the Veil the one time she couldn't accompany me, but I was also resigned to traveling alone if need be.

"Then when I actually saw the roaming Veil and realized I wan't too late, my heart cracked because of what it meant. I would be crossing the Veil to find my brother and in the process, would be leaving behind my sister *and* my newly found mate.

"Though I now suspect fate had something to do with your presence there that day, thank you for not giving up, for coming after me and for latching on as I went through the Veil. I cannot imagine living this life, cut off from Faerie, without you."

"I feel the same, my love. I think of those moments

when I saw you for the first time and knew you for my mate, and remember how I panicked. I was terrified I was going to lose you right when I found you, and I give thanks every day for the miracle that is you, and of course, for your forgiving nature."

Luna giggled again. "You were rather obnoxious, but in the end, you were also perfect for me."

Ah, Luna, so were you for me, my love. So were you for me. With that, he kissed her and rolled her beneath him, kissing her still.

For the next several hours, there were no more words spoken. Instead, the night air was filled with heat and passion and endless, enduring love.

Read on for an excerpt from ZARA.

Zara's heart was pounding and she felt as if she couldn't catch her breath.

The Fae she'd come to the palace to heal, the *Crown Prince of Faerie* himself, was her *mate*.

Her unbelievably gorgeous, sexy-as-sin, *fated mate*.

This couldn't be right.

It just couldn't.

She was an ordinary Fae, nothing special about her at all.

She might have an affinity for life magic, of such magnitude that her parents had insisted she not demonstrate her power in public, but that didn't mean she was powerful enough to become a Crown Princess.

It was insane.

Absolute madness.

Panic rising, Zara went to take a step back, but Zivek lunged upward, catching her hand in his and pulling her onto the bed beside him.

Queen Naira raised an eyebrow at the two of them. "I'm sorry. Do you two already know each other?"

Zivek grinned and slung an arm around Zara's shoulders. "Mother, this is Zara. Zara, my mother."

"Yeah, I got that," Zara said. "Your mother, the *Queen* of Faerie."

Zivek chuckled, then added, "Mother, Zara is my mate."

Panic exploded inside Zara even as Queen Naira's face lit with joy.

"No, no, no," Zara said, waving her hand in a frantic attempt to ward off the army of words she was certain the Queen was about to speak, words that might welcome her into the Royal family, that might doom her as a future queen of Faerie. "No, that's not right."

Zivek gave her an incredulous look. "Are you seriously about to deny that we're mates?"

"It's just that–that–" Zara searched frantically for a reason, *any* reason, that would get her out of this terrible turn of events that might end with her being crowned queen.

"Zivek, are you certain?" Queen Naira asked, a look of concern on her face, probably because no one in their right mind would deny their fated mate.

"I heard her voice inside me." Zivek stared into Zara's eyes. "Your voice pulled me from the dark."

"Yes, but you're the Crown Prince of Faerie," Zara exclaimed. "Besides, your name is Zivek," she burst out.

He raised an eyebrow. "It is."

"Zara and Zivek? It sounds ridiculous."

"You're objecting because of our names?" There was an adorable look of confusion on his face, as if he couldn't quite understand how they'd arrived at this point.

"Well, yes?" Zara cleared her throat, then repeated with greater force. "*Yes*. You cannot possibly wish to be announced as Prince Zivek and Princess Zara everywhere we go. Surely you understand."

Find out what happens next in ZARA.

THE MURRYSVILLE COALITION

The Crazy Cheetah Lady

One Sad Kitty

A PAWSITIVELY PURRFECT MATCH

Catnapped

The Real McCat

Unbearably Cute

A Catmas to Remember

This Cat's for You

Santa Kitty

Hocus Purrcus

Tridents & Tails

Abra-Cat-Abra

Satan's Kitty

Valen-Cats

Vampurr Lovin'

A Beautiful Cat-ship

Grave Cattitude

THE SHENANIGANS SERIES

Shifter Shenanigans

Witchy Shenanigans

Full Moon Shenanigans

Hotel Shenanigans

Dragon Shenanigans

Undercover Shenanigans

Spooky Shenanigans

Holiday Shenanigans

Valentine Shenanigans

Lucky Shenanigans

STORIES OF THE VEIL

Guardians of the Veil

Astra

Glory

Luna

Zara

Lotus

WICKED

No Rest for the Wicked

Wicked Is As Wicked Does

PAWSITIVELY PURRFECT TRILOGIES

THE CAT'S MEOW

Catnapped | The Real McCat | Unbearably Cute

HOLLY JOLLY PAWLIDAY

A Catmas to Remember | This Cat's for You | Santa Kitty

SHENANIGANS ANTHOLOGIES

CRAZED

Books 1-3

AMAZED

Books 4-6

HOLIDAZED

Books 7-10

SHENANIGANS

The Complete Collection

STORIES OF THE VEIL

THE UNVEILED

Astra | Glory

THE VEILED

Luna | Zara

WICKED DUET

WICKED

No Rest for the Wicked | Wicked Is As Wicked Does

ABOUT THE AUTHOR

WWW.PEPPERMCGRAW.COM

PEPPER MCGRAW is a *USA Today* Bestselling Author of paranormal romance. She hasn't met any paranormals to date, but she's sure that moment is just around the corner!

Pepper loves animals, especially cats, and spends her free time volunteering at local shelters and for Trap-Neuter-Release programs.

She's had the supreme honor of winning occasional head butts and meows from the local ferals in her neighborhood and has even convinced a few to come inside and adopt her for their very own.

bookbub.com/authors/pepper-mcgraw
facebook.com/ShenanigansSeries
goodreads.com/peppermcgraw
instagram.com/peppermcgraw_author
tiktok.com/@peppermcgraw
twitter.com/peppermcgraw